The Forgotten Things

Written and Illustrated by

ANDREW MAHAN

PAGE PUBLISHING, INC.
New York, NY

First originally published by Page Publishing, Inc. 2016

ISBN 978-1-68289-370-8 (pbk)
ISBN 978-1-68289-371-5 (digital)

Printed in the United States of America

Dedication

This book is dedicated to my "Tinkerbell" Cheryl,
"Wendy Lady" Anne, "RED", and my family

2016

Not far from where you live, just down the street, and around the corner, there sits a small stone building with round windows and a bright pink door. It's called "The Little Shop" and I am its owner. In my shop there are all kinds of toys. There are baby dolls, dinosaurs, marionettes, teddy bears, and even cars that drive, and planes that fly. There are also older toys in my shop. These toys are brought to my shop because their owners no longer want them or don't like them anymore. Although they don't look like much to most people, these broken Forgotten Things are extra special indeed. I would like to tell you about a few of them if you have the time. Maybe then you will see just how special they are.

The Patchwork Teddy Bear

Who Forgot How to Hug

There once was a teddy bear who sat on a shelf all alone and sad. He was not the cutest of bears, in fact he was quite a sad sight to behold. One eye was glass, the other was button, and he had only one ear and a patch where the other ear used to be. He had lost most of the stuffing in his body so his head was too big and weighed him down, and he had patches all over including a big red heart patch on his chest. While all the other stuffed animals sat with their arms open ready to give a big hug, the Patchwork Teddy Bear sat with his arms down to his side afraid to even try. How did he get this way you ask? Let me tell you how.

Years ago, the Bear was given to a little boy by his grandmother for his birthday. The boy was kind at first and took care of the Bear and even held him at night. But as the boy grew older he became mean and began playing too rough with the Bear. He would beat him up, throw him around, and even stepped on him a time or two, then when he was tired of the Bear he gave him to his dog as a chew toy. One day, the grandma came for a visit and saw the poor Bear lying on the ground all chewed and torn. She reached down, picked the bear up, and walked to the trash can. But before she threw him in she looked at his face. One ear had been torn off, and one eye was missing, he had lost most of his stuffing, and had tears all over his body, but for some reason she just couldn't throw him away.

"I think you still have a few hugs left in you," she said and with that she took him home and began to sew him up. She gave him new stuffing and a new button eye. She sewed up the holes and tears, and covered them with different color patches. Lastly, she

covered a large hole on his chest with a big red heart patch. Then she kissed him on the head and took him to The Little Shop. There he was placed on a shelf with many other stuffed animals that were much newer than him. Every day children would come and run over to the shelf and begin hugging every stuffed animal trying to find the one that fit in their arms just right. But no one ever hugged the Patchwork Teddy Bear. One by one the new stuffed animals were bought and slowly the shelf became more and more empty. One day, the bear began to cry.

"*No one will ever buy me. My first boy didn't want me either,*" he said with tears streaming down his face. "*I must have done something wrong.*"

Just then the Patchwork Teddy Bear heard a soft gentle voice come from the other side of the shelf.

"*That's not true. He just couldn't see how wonderful you are.*"

The bear turned his head and there, sitting on the shelf beside him, was a little stuffed owl. She was short and round, and only had one wing, and one of her eyes was green and the other was blue.

"*You did nothing wrong little bear,*" she said. "*That boy just didn't know what love really is. You will find someone who will love you.*"

The Patchwork Teddy Bear lowered his head and said, "*I don't think so. I don't even remember how to hug. No one wants a bear who can't hug.*"

The little owl just smiled and said, "*You haven't forgotten how to hug, you're just out of practice. I'll bet your hug is super extra special. You just need to find someone who deserves such a special hug.*"

At that moment the door to The Little Shop opened and a woman walked in. She slowly made her way over to the shelf where the stuffed animals sat and began taking the best and cutest looking stuffed animals and placing them in a large basket. When she got to the Patchwork Teddy Bear, she stopped. She looked at him for a moment then tilted her head and smiled.

"*You remind me of someone very special. He's sad too. He needs a friend and I think you are the perfect match.*"

The kind woman took the Patchwork Teddy Bear, and the little owl and several other stuffed animals, and bought them. She then drove to a large white building where many sick people were. The kind woman took the stuffed animals inside, up an elevator, and down a long hall until she reached a big room where there were children lying in beds. One by one the kind woman gave each child a stuffed animal. The little owl went to a little girl who only had one arm.

"She's just like you," the Patchwork Teddy Bear said as the girl hugged the little owl tightly. Then the kind woman walked to the end of the room to the very last bed where a little boy was sitting looking out the window. He was very small and thin, and had many machines and tubes attached to him. He had no hair, and his skin was blotchy and looked like he had patches all over his body.

"He looks like me," the Patchwork Teddy Bear thought as the woman walked over to the boy.

"I brought you a friend," the woman said, *"He may not look like much but I think he just needs someone to love him."*

The boy looked at the Bear for a moment. He saw the patches on its body, the button eye, and the missing ear. Then he touched the big red heart patch on the Bear's chest. The boy smiled and scooped the bear up into his arms. *"I'll take care of you,"* the boy whispered into the Bear's one ear. The Patchwork Teddy Bear froze for a moment not knowing what to do and then he did something he hadn't done in a long time, he smiled and wrapped his patchwork arms around the little boy in a super extra special hug.

"Every heart is made to love, and everyone's arms were created to hug. You just have to find the one who deserves your super extra special hug."

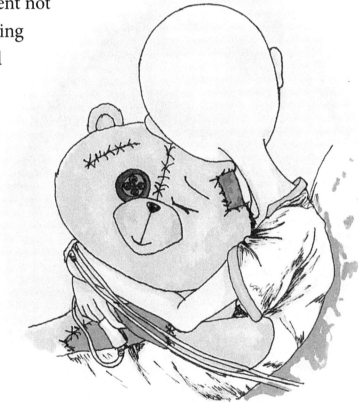

6

The Clown

That Lost His Smile

Have you ever met a clown who didn't know how to smile? I have. Where you ask? Why at my shop of course. You see the little clown used to belong to a girl who loved him very much and took wonderful care of him for he was her best friend in the whole world. As the girl grew up, her love for the clown only grew stronger. He remained on her dresser as she went to school, then to college. He was even there when she and her husband came home together for the first time. Then one day, the little girl who was all grown up left for work like she did every day, but this time she didn't come back. The clown waited and waited as the days passed, but still she didn't come home. Then one morning, the woman's husband came upstairs to their room, picked up the clown, and took him downstairs. There he was placed on a large black box next to a picture of his friend. The clown looked around and saw many people dressed in black all crying and looking very sad. The clown didn't know what was going on but deep inside he knew that he would never see his best friend again. The next day, the woman's husband took the clown and put him in a box with many other of the woman's belongings and brought them to a little shop down the street. There, the clown was placed on a shelf with many other clowns of all shapes and sizes. The other clowns all had big smiles and joyful faces but not him. His heart was so sad that he couldn't smile even when he tried.

"*I've lost my smile,*" he said.

"*That's nonsense,*" said a jester with a big painted smile on his face. "*You can't lose a smile. You're a clown. You're created to smile and make people laugh.*"

"How can I?" said the clown. *"I've lost my best friend in the whole world."*

The jester just shrugged, *"It's easy you just…smile!"*

The clown lifted his head and tried to smile, but then he thought about the black box and how he would never see his friend again and his smile faded back into a frown. The jester became very frustrated and finally gave up all together. The little clown buried his face in his knees and closed his eyes. Later that night right before The Little Shop was about to close, three nurses walked in. They began looking around until they came to the shelf where the clowns sat. They began laughing and smiling as they picked up each clown and commented on how cute they were. Then one of the nurses saw one clown sitting all alone in the corner. She reached over and gently picked him up and held him in her arms.

"Why so sad little one?" she asked. *"There is so much to smile about. Here let me show you."*

The three nurses left the store with the little clown and a few others and drove to a big building filled with people. The nurses took the clown to a small room where several cribs were and sat the clown down inside a crib next to a crying new born baby girl. The girl stared at the clown sitting at her feet and her eyes got big. The clown was afraid the girl would start to cry so he whispered, *"Hello,"* and managed a tiny smile. The girl burst into a smile and began to giggle with joy. The clown's heart grew warm and his tiny smile soon turned into a full smile that stretched across his face. As the girl continued to laugh the clown began laughing with her and soon all the babies and even the nurses in the room were giggling with joy at the clown and his smile. From then on each day was filled with a dozen new hellos and the only tears were tears of joy.

"For every goodbye there is a new hello.
For every cloud there is a rainbow. Look for the rainbows."

The Doll

With the Yellow Yarn Hair

In my shop there once stood a little vanity and on that vanity stood many beautiful dolls. There was a cheerleading doll, a doctor doll, and even a rock and roll doll. The most beautiful dolls however were the three porcelain dolls that stood in the middle of the vanity. Their hair was perfect, and each of them wore a lovely ball gown with long white gloves. The last doll that sat on the shelf was not made of beautiful porcelain and she didn't wear a lovely ball gown with white gloves. She was simple, with a little purple dress with lace, two button eyes, a sewn on smile, and bright yellow yarn for hair. Every morning the other dolls would brush their hair so it looked perfect when the children arrived. The doll with the yarn hair would watch them intently in awe of their beauty.

"Your hair is so lovely," she would say. *"How wonderful it must be to be so pretty."*

The other dolls would just smirk and reply, *"Yes, it is wonderful being pretty."*

"I would love to wear a beautiful ball gown like yours," the doll with the yarn hair said with a smile.

One of the porcelain dolls turned and looked at the doll with the yarn hair and said, *"These dresses are meant for pretty dolls with pretty faces. You wouldn't look right in one. You see, you're just too plain."*

The other dolls went back to brushing their hair as the doll with the yarn hair sat back down and quietly watched. That night, as all the toys slept, the doll with the yarn hair sat looking in the large mirror where the other dolls stand and brush their hair. She imaged that she was a pretty porcelain doll with a lovely ball gown and white

12

gloves and she danced and twirled around. Then she saw one of the hair brushes that the other dolls used. She picked it up and began brushing her yarn hair pretending it too was beautiful and flowing like the other dolls. While she was brushing her yarn hair however the brush got caught. She tried to get it out but it had caught in her thick yarn hair. She pulled with all her might and finally with a loud *"Riiiiiip!"* the brush came out and with it, some of her yellow yarn hair. The doll looked in the mirror at the large bald patch on her head and began to cry, *"I'm not plain, I'm ugly."*

The next morning, as the other dolls brushed their hair, they laughed at her and called her names. When the store opened a little girl with straw colored hair and her father walked in. He led her over to the vanity where the dolls all stood and told her that she could pick one doll to take home. The little girl looked at each doll very carefully. When she got to the porcelain dolls she admired their lovely dresses and perfect hair.

"Would you like one of those dolls, sweet pea?" the girl's father asked.

The girl thought for a moment then responded, *"No, they're pretty but they're just meant to be looked at."* The little girl looked around at all the dolls then stopped when she saw the doll with the yarn hair sitting by the mirror. The girl picked her up and looked at her face with the button eyes and sewn on smile.

"You don't want me," the doll said, *"I'm ugly."*

"I like this one, daddy," the girl said with a smile.

"Are you sure? Wouldn't you rather have one of the pretty porcelain dolls?"

The little girl just looked at the doll with the yarn hair and smiled even brighter, *"Those dolls are very pretty, yes, but this doll is beautiful."* Then she hugged the doll tightly and smiled a big smile. *"I think you are the most beautiful dolly that ever was."* As the little girl with the straw colored hair held her, the dolly with the yarn hair closed her eyes and thought, *"I'm beautiful."*

"There is no such thing as plain.
There is beauty in all of us, you just have to learn how to see it."

13

15

The Ballerina

Who Couldn't Turn

On the floor in the darkest corner of my shop, there once sat a beautiful ballerina doll. She had a lovely pink tutu and beautiful brown hair all tied up in a bun. Why was she on the floor you ask? Well she was broken, you see. When the ballerina was bought from a big toy store all beautifully packaged and new, she had only one leg. Because she only had one leg she couldn't leap, or stand on her toes, or turn in lovely pirouettes like all ballet dolls should. The people that bought her wondered how a toy company could make such a mistake. She was then brought here to the little shop because they didn't want a "broken" ballerina. The ballerina felt ashamed and so she hid behind an old doll house that sat in the corner.

"Why was I made this way?" the ballerina would ask with tears in her eyes. *"What good is a ballerina who cannot turn? Why am I broken?"*

At that moment a young girl and her parents walked into the little shop. The ballerina watched through one of the windows in the dollhouse as the family walked around the store looking at every toy, stuffed animal, and doll. When the young girl got close to where the ballerina was, she stopped to look at a china doll sitting on the shelf above the dollhouse. As the girl was holding the china doll, she knocked over a few blocks that fell behind the dollhouse. The young girl put the china doll down and moved the dollhouse to retrieve the blocks, and as she did she saw something very special. There behind the dollhouse was a beautiful ballerina doll with a lovely pink tutu and beautiful brown hair.

"Why are you down here?" The young girl asked as she held the ballerina and fixed her tutu. *"Mamma, may I please get the ballerina?"* The girl asked.

Her mother walked over to her and looked at the ballerina and said, *"Are you sure you want her, sweetie? She is broken."*

The young girl shook her head, *"She's not broken, she's just missing a piece."*

The ballerina's heart was filled with such joy and excitement, *"She's going to fix me,"* she thought. *"I will finally be a real ballerina."*

The young girl and her family took the ballerina home and as soon as they got there the young girl took the ballerina upstairs to her room. *"I know exactly what you need, my beautiful ballerina. Your missing piece."*

The young girl walked over to her dresser and stood the ballerina up on her one foot and then placed her hand in someone else's. The ballerina looked up and there standing in front of her was a beautiful boy ballet dancer who only had one arm.

"He's missing a piece too. I've been looking for it for a long time," the young girl said with a smile. *"It's you. Now you can both dance."*

The little girl's mother called her down for dinner and she ran downstairs. The ballerina looked at the boy ballet dancer shyly, *"I've never really danced before. I've never been able to."*

The boy ballet dancer just smiled and held her hand tightly, *"I'll help you."* Then they began to dance and together they turned in lovely pirouettes.

"Everyone has a purpose, a place that no one else
can fill as perfectly as you."

19

The Unicorn

That Tried to Hide His Colors

Once upon a time there lived a unicorn. No, this unicorn didn't live in a fairy tale land. He lived in my shop. He was all white with a shimmering rainbow mane and tail, and a golden horn on the top of his head. Being the only unicorn toy in the store he was often teased by the other horse toys.

"You're weird," they would say. *"You should be ashamed of yourself being all shimmery and colorful. It's not normal."*

"But my bright colors and shimmer make me special," the Unicorn said.

"You're not special, you're unnatural. We are normal 'real' horses. No one is going to want to buy something like you."

One night, the Unicorn was so sad from all the teasing and hurtful words that he couldn't sleep at all. He took a walk around the little shop and ended up by the front door where he saw the muddy welcome mat. The Unicorn had an idea.

"Maybe if I change the way I look the other horses will like me more."

The Unicorn rolled around on the mat until all his beautiful colors were covered in mud. The next morning the other horses acted much nicer because the Unicorn looked and acted like them. Deep in his heart the Unicorn didn't feel right.

"I miss my colors," he thought but, still, he kept himself covered with mud. The next day a young boy walked into the store with his mom. He was very shy and quiet as he walked over to the horses. He looked at all the horses of every shape, size, and color, but nothing seemed to interest him. Then the boy saw something strange. There in the middle of all the other horses stood a muddy brown horse with a horn on the

top of his head. When he picked up the horse, he noticed some gold paint peeking through the brown on his horn. The boy scraped some of the brown mud off and revealed the bright gold underneath.

"You poor thing, you're all dirty. Why would anyone want to cover you up?" The boy bought the unicorn and took him home where he began giving him a bath in the sink. *"I know what it's like to be different,"* the boy said as he lovingly scrubbed the dirt off of the unicorn's face. *"At school I'm teased because I don't like to play any of the sports in gym, and I like playing with horses and stuffed animals instead of soldiers and cars. The other boys call me names but I know I'm just like you, different. I think you're more beautiful than any regular old horse. I think you're very special. Just like me. Promise me you'll never try to hide all your beautiful colors again,"* the boy said lovingly. The now clean unicorn smiled and whispered, *"As long as you never hide yours."*

"Never let anyone dull your sparkle."

The Marionette

With the Broken Strings

In my shop there is a place where all the toys that are a little odd, or are missing pieces, or just plain don't fit in anywhere else in the store, are placed. Toys like rubber ducks that can't squeak, and bouncy balls that cant bounce, yo-yo's without strings, and letter blocks like "Q" without a "U" to stand beside it. In that same corner, there once sat a boy marionette. Why, you ask, was he in the misfit corner? Well he was at one time on the shelf with the other puppets and marionettes waiting for someone to come and buy him. Then there came a day when a wicked child entered The Little Shop and began playing very harshly with all the toys. When he got to the marionette boy he took him by the strings and tossed him around in the air and threw him at the wall causing one of his legs to break.

The wicked child then tore off the marionettes clothes and threw them on the ground. The last thing the wicked child did was break the marionette boy's strings and laugh as he walked away. One of the women who worked at The Little Shop found the now incomplete marionette boy and took him to the corner where the other incomplete and odd toys were. The marionette boy looked at his hands and feet where his strings used to be and he began to cry.

"I will never dance or play again," he said, *"What did I do that would make him hurt me?"*

As the marionette boy sat and cried as hard as he could, the rubber ducky who couldn't squeak moved closer to him.

"*You didn't do anything wrong, sweet boy,*" he said softly. "*Sometimes people do mean and awful things never thinking about who they might hurt. I'm sorry you ended up in this part of the shop with all of us broken toys.*"

The marionette boy brushed off a tear and looked around at all the misfit toys around him. "*But you're all still good toys. You may not be able to squeak anymore but I'm sure you can still float in a bath. I should just be thrown away. I'm ruined. I'm worthless.*"

One night the marionette decided he was going to throw himself in the trash. "*No one will miss me,*" he said sadly. "*I might as well just not be.*" And with that he jumped off the shelf and into the trash can sitting below.

The next day a young man came into The Little Shop. He slowly made his way around the store and finally ended up at the corner where the misfit toys were. He stopped and carefully looked at each toy intently. Then he noticed the marionette boy sitting in the trash can. He knelt down, reached in, and pulled the marionette boy out. The young man's eyes were kind and sweet as he looked at the marionette boy and smiled, "*You are just what I've been looking for.*"

The marionette boy just stared in confusion, "*But I'm ruined. You don't want me.*"

But the young man took the marionette boy anyway as well as all the other misfit toys to his home. He then took the misfit toys to his workshop where he began to fix them. He gave the rubber duck a new squeaker, he patched up the bouncy ball and filled it with air, he gave the yo-yo a new string, and he made a "U" block for the lonely "Q." When he got to the marionette boy he took special care as he painted him up like new, mended his broken leg, made him beautiful new clothes, and threaded new strings into his hands and feet.

He then placed a small golden crown on the marionette boy's head saying, "*You are very important little prince. You are just who I've been needing.*"

That night, the young man took the no longer misfit toys, with many other toys he had, to a small brick building where inside there were many people dressed in old and torn clothes, with dirty hands and faces.

"*This must be the place where misfit people are kept,*" the marionette boy thought. The young man then took the toys to a group of children where he carefully chose one child to give each toy to, except for the marionette boy. The young man took the marionette boy and several other marionettes he had with him to a little wooden puppet stage where he then told the story of a brave prince who saved the land from a fierce dragon. The marionette boy filled with joy and pride as the children watched, laughed, and cheered when the little marionette prince danced and played.

"No one will ever hurt you again," the young man said. "You are brave and strong."

"Nothing is so broken that it cannot be mended."

The Chubby Dinosaur

Who Just Wanted a Friend

On the floor in my shop there once sat a very chubby dinosaur. She did not look like the other dinosaur toys who were very realistic looking with sharp claws and teeth. She was not made of plastic, instead she was stuffed, and very large, and was bright pink and green. She was new to the store and was excited to make friends with the other dinosaur toys. But no matter how nice she was the other dinosaurs didn't want to be friends. Instead they began to make fun of the chubby dinosaur and call her names like *"Fattysaur"* and *"Chubbysaurus."* The T-rex said that the chubby dinosaur was so big that there was hardly enough room for all of them to fit in The Little Shop. The chubby dinosaur didn't understand why they were all being so mean when she just wanted to be friends. The next day, as children came and began to play with the toys, the chubby dinosaur watched as the other dinosaurs roared and growled, scaring her and the other toys.

"Why are you scaring everyone?" She asked.

"Because we're dinosaurs, we're supposed to be scary," said the T-rex. *"Chubby dinosaurs like you will never be scary or tough. Everyone would just laugh at you. They already laugh at you because that's what you do to chubby things."*

Days went by and the other dinosaurs continued to scare all the other toys and tease the chubby dinosaur. Then one day a very timid boy and his father walked into the little shop. When he saw the dinosaurs he got very excited and he ran right over. The realistic dinosaurs were too scary for him so he quickly began to walk away.

That's when he walked right up to the chubby dinosaur who was almost as tall as he was. The chubby dinosaur became very nervous.

"He seems like such a nice boy, I hope I don't scare him," she thought. The timid boy slowly raised his hand and petted the top of the chubby dinosaur's head. She was very soft and warm. The boy let out a quiet giggle and threw his arms around the chubby dinosaur's neck. That day the chubby dinosaur went home with the boy and his dad. And later that night, the boy's father read him and the chubby dinosaur a wonderful bedtime story. Then the father told the boy, *"It's time for bed."*

And after the boy's father gave him a kiss on the head, he turned out the light and walked out of the room. The timid boy pulled his covers over his face and became very afraid.

"I'm scared of the dark," the boy said. *"I'm scared that there's a monster under my bed."*

The chubby dinosaur looked at the frightened boy and thought of how scared she was when the other dinosaurs would growl and roar.

"Maybe chubby dinosaurs can be brave and tough too."

Then the chubby dinosaur stretched her neck as high as she could and let out a growl, *"I am bigger and tougher than any bed monsters. No one will hurt my new friend."*

"No one can tell you who you are or what you can and can't do.
That power lies only within you."

The Baby Doll

That Thought She Was Ugly

In my shop there is a shelf where dozens of baby dolls sit. We have every shape and size, some with brown eyes, blue eyes, dark hair, light hair, even boy and girl dolls. Some of them burp, some cry mamma, and some even wet their diapers. One baby doll in particular was very different from the rest, for she was the only baby doll in the whole shop with dark skin. Some of the other baby dolls treated her badly because she was different from them. The rest of the baby dolls didn't know what to think so they just stayed quiet when the other dolls made fun of her and called her names.

"Just look at her," one of the mean baby dolls said. *"Who would ever want an ugly doll like her?"*

The baby doll with the dark skin would often cry herself to sleep because she didn't understand why the other dolls were so mean to her. One night one of the smaller boy dolls came and sat beside her.

"I'm sorry the other dolls are so mean to you. I don't see what they're talking about. You have two eyes just like the rest of us, two hands, two feet, and a nose just like we do. I think you're beautiful."

The baby doll with the dark skin brushed away her tears and managed a smile. *"Thank you,"* she said softly. That night the boy doll and the baby doll with the dark skin talked for hours about their favorite colors and what makes them smile. The next morning the other dolls began their teasing again only this time they were teasing the boy doll as well.

"Be careful or no one will buy you if they see you sitting with her."

"Be nice!" The boy doll said defending his friend. *"You're the one no one will buy. No one wants a mean baby doll."*

The dolls were so busy arguing that they didn't even notice the young girl walking toward them until she was standing right in front of the shelf.

"Look at all the baby dolls," the girl said with a sweet smile.

The dolls all stopped fighting and put on their best smiles hoping to be chosen to be taken home by the young girl. She slowly made her way down the line, looking at every baby doll very carefully. Before she could get to the baby doll with the dark skin however one of the mean dolls pushed her off the shelf. The boy doll tried to stop her but it was too late and the baby doll with the dark skin began falling to the floor. The young girl reached the end of the line and her smile turned into a frown. It seemed she hadn't found what she was looking for. The young girl lowered her head and turned to walk away. As she did her eye caught something that had fallen behind a cardboard box on the floor. She bent down and pulled out a beautiful baby doll with dark skin. Her eyes got big and a smile stretched across her face.

"Look, mommy, a dolly that looks like me," the young girl said as she gently touched the baby doll's face, and began to rock her in her arms. *"You look sad. Don't be sad, little baby, I'll take care of you. My mommy says not to be sad because you're different. She tells me something every day that makes me feel better. Maybe it will make you feel better too. You are beautiful, and special, and important, just like me."* As the young girl continued to rock her, the baby doll closed her eyes and thought about the words the girl said. *"I am beautiful, and special, and important."*

"No matter what anyone ever tells you or how anyone makes you feel, just remember that you are beautiful, special, and important."

Never judge a book by its cover or a teddy bear by its patches, because where some people who might see a tattered old bear, someone else sees a super extra special friend with a big heart. So the next time you look in the mirror and feel plain, think of the doll with yellow yarn hair who wanted to be pretty all while being the most beautiful dolly in the world. Or if you feel broken and worthless, remember the marionette boy and know that you are worth far too much to be thrown away. And if ever you feel ugly, think about the baby doll with the dark skin and remember that you too are beautiful, special, and important.

About the Author

ndrew Mahan was born in Rockford, Illinois, to Ellen and Bob Mahan. He grew up on the upper west side along with his brother Micah, sister Megan, and grandmother Sandy. Early in his life, art became is favorite outlet. It became his only way of coping and healing until later in life when he would develop a love of writing, dancing, and singing. After high school, Andrew began a career both as a principal dancer for several dance and theater companies as well as a featured soloist with orchestras from around the Greater Chicago area. Andrew has worked as a choreographer for several youth, community, and professional theater companies as well as some local high schools in his home town of Rockford. In 2012, Andrew and his mother Ellen opened Gateway Performing Arts Studio in Rockford as a way of using their passions to inspire and educate students in the arts. In 2010, Andrew began writing *The Forgotten Things*, which is actually a collection of stories based on Andrew's own life. As a child, Andrew was a victim of molestation. Then through childhood, middle school, and high school, Andrew was bullied both verbally and physically for the way he looked, talked, and any other reason people could find. Andrew's desire through his writing is to give words to those who are too scared to speak and hope to those who feel as though they have none. After all, "There is nothing so broken, that it cannot be mended."

CPSIA information can be obtained
at www.ICGtesting.com
Printed in the USA
LVOW05s0043200116

471424LV00030B/335/P